THE SACKCLOTH HEROES OF JUNIPER

BOOK ONE

THE BERRYSBORO BRAWL

BLAKE VERBOOM

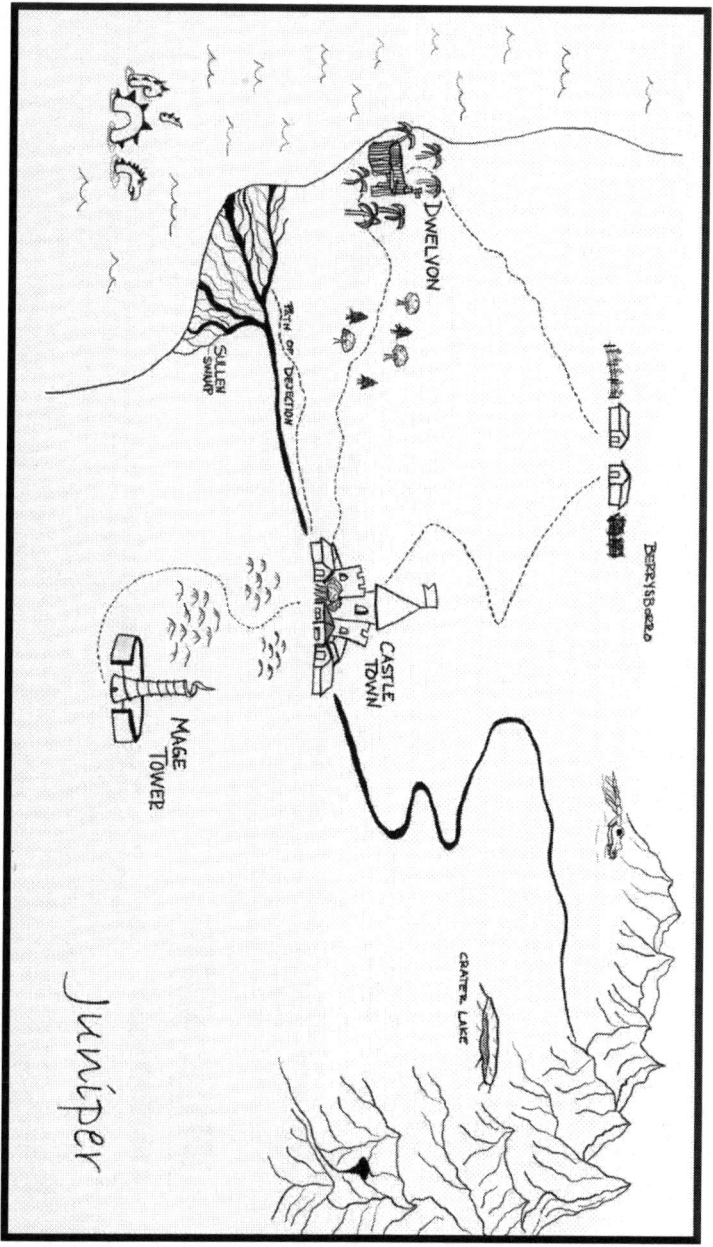

Juniper

This book is dedicated to my best friend, my biggest supporter, my loving wife.

And to all of my friends who listened, advised and encouraged me along the way.

CONTENTS

BOOK ONE

THE BERRYSBORO
BRAWL

Chapter 1

THE END OF THE BEGINNING

"To the pit! To the pit with them!"

The horde of sweaty, stinking peasants prodded us with pitchforks. Our backs edged toward a plank that stood above a festering pit – home to some unknown, hideous threat.

"Please, listen to us!" Borzun shouted. "This is all a big misunderstanding!" My dwarf friend was right, but he wouldn't be the one to convince this crowd.

"Don't listen to 'em!" A burly peasant yelled back. "He's full of mischief that one is!"

"Yarr!" The rest of the mob let their chorus resound. "To the pit with them!"

"No! Please..." Duncan the wizard fell to his knees. "I have too much to live for! I— "

"Ah, shut up!" A skinny, old man yelled. "To the pit!"

"To the pit!" They echoed.

"Well go on then!" Olivander the elf bellowed. "Take us if you must. But at least tell us what we're in for!"

"Aye, what's in this blasted pit of yours?" I said, strengthening my resolve.

An oafish peasant stepped forward with a raised torch. He grinned broadly, exposing large, brown teeth. "Beehtwuls!" He said. The crowd fell silent and somewhere a cricket chirped.

"What?" I asked.

"Ahem," he cleared his throat. "Beehtwuls..."

"Beehtwuls? What kind of beast is that?"

"Y'know... a beehtwul. Lil' shiny things. 'Ard shells n' clicky wings."

"You mean beetles?"

"Aye! Beehtwuls!"

Duncan stood. "Are they poisonous?" He asked.

"Wellll..." Another peasant stepped forward. "Not exactly."

"Do they have pinchers?" Borzun raised an

eyebrow. The crowd let out a murmur and the man turned to consult with them.

"Some of 'em probably do!" Said the peasant as he faced us again.

"Well that's not so bad then," Olivander shrugged.

"Oy!" An old woman stepped forward from the mob. "You say that now! We'll see what you say when you've been in a pit with filthy, stinking beetles crawlin' all over you for three days! Besides, we're naught but simple villagers... it's the best we could do." Her head drooped and an old man patted her shoulder.

"Yah! That's right!" A skinny serf with a leather cap added. "An' I threw me garbage in there two days ago! You'll see!"

"Blast it, Milton!" Someone shouted. "You know you're not supposed ta' throw your garbage in the pit!" Milton shrank back as the crowd uttered disapproval.

"Enough of this!" The burly one growled. "To the pit!"

"Yarr!" the crowd shouted again and pressed in on us. I could feel my Adam's apple scrape my throat as I gulped.

Mercy me! How did it come to this?

Even as the thought came, my life seemed to flash before my eyes...

Chapter 2

THE BEGINNING

Wind swept through my hair and flew across the dry countryside. In Juniper, where the wind blows, the dust follows. I shielded my eyes and pressed on toward my prize. Red sand swirled and surrounded me as I lifted the steel ring attached to the great-wood door. I let it fall three times. Each motion produced a resounding thud. Creaking, almost cracking, the door inched open and an estate guard peered at me.

"Summon the master," I said. The guard nodded and disappeared. The minute that passed seemed to be an hour. Finally, the door swept open and there stood the master. A fine leather cape draped over his broad shoulders, and a thin silver circlet lined his dominant brow with grace. He was certainly a man of magnitude.

"Master, it is an honor to stand before you." I pulled my sword from its sheath and knelt.

"Aye lad, and why is it you call on me? The hour is late and I have much to do even still," the master said.

"Indeed, and it is not my intention to waste your time," I replied. "Good master, there are not many who know what I am about to tell you. Juniper, our beloved land, is falling once more on dark times. Rumblings stir from the south and black clouds are rolling from the north. Our allies to the west can aid us no more, and there are those who have again heard the evil whisperings – they say the Sorcerer of Ungvar is returning. Never before have we been so threatened. Master, I feel this in my bones. Now, more than ever, Juniper needs a champion, and I would pledge my sword to you."

I held my sword flat across both palms of my hands. Only the wind spoke. I gulped and resisted the urge to shuffle. Eventually, I had to look up. The master stared at me, his gaze piercing downward. He rubbed his chin and his mouth twisted oddly. Just as I thought I could bear it no longer, a steady smile crept across his face. Hope began to well within my chest! Once more I knew what it meant to be proud. Finally, finally I had found—

"Bwahahahaha! Oho! Aha! Ohhhhhhh…" The master slapped his knees as tears streamed down his face. "Genie! I say, Genie come here! GENIE!"

"Yes?" A woman appeared in an extravagant dress. "What is it Reg?"

"Listen to this, listen to… ahahaha! Just listen! Lad, do it again – do the act again."

"It's not an act…" I stood and sheathed my blade. "I meant everything I said. Dire times await!"

"Bwahaha! Did y'hear!?" The master said.

"Oh please, please do it again!" The woman smiled and waited.

"No! I will not be made a mockery of…"

"Ohhh, ah! It's okay, I understand lad. I'm sure you do this for a living. Take this and let the guard know when your next show is, we'll surely be there!" The master flipped a coin at me and walked away with an arm around his wife. "Oh Genie, you shoulda heard him! He did this hilarious comedy about black clouds and evil sorcerers in Juniper again, ahaha! Can you

6

believe that!?"

BOOM – the heavy door shook dust from its frame as it closed. My feet dragged across the cracked ground as I gradually made my way to the hitching post. I untied my noble steed, Punter, and we drifted toward the heart of town.

"Well buddy, at least we have enough for a meal tonight." I held up the silver coin the master had given me as I rubbed Punter's snout.

Bulwark was the name of the town where we stayed. Once it was famed for the many successful war-time defenses it had given to our people. But now, it was little more than a glorified theatre. Everywhere you looked, some performance was ongoing. People gathered in droves to hear tales of our land as it used to be. I listened as I passed by one such performance.

"The most dangerous foe Juniper ever saw had now breached the castle gates," the silver-haired storyteller bellowed. "Ryth'Gar Roksinge and his band of wizard-warriors were poised outside the throne room when our great King enacted his dire plan. He locked himself in battle with Ryth'Gar! Single combat, to the death, he said! But our king knew that he could not prevail against such an enemy. Seizing his opportunity, King Junip the Eleventh, pounced and clung to his adversary! Then... even as Ryth'Gar was about to give a fatal strike, our King gave the order... our own wizard champion, the now-great Archmage Fardron, launched an engulfing fireball at them both. The King held Ryth'Gar long enough to keep him from defending."

The storyteller paused and I saw a sad sparkle in his eye. "The explosion was devastating. Neither Ryth'Gar, nor the King, were ever seen again. Leaderless, the enemy fled, and order was restored to Castletown and Juniper alike."

Applause erupted from the crowd. They clapped, cheered, whooped and whistled. But the storyteller remained somber. His audience left without delay. They slurped chilled beverages and smacked toasted snacks as they rushed off, undoubtedly to find the next source of entertainment.

"I enjoyed your story sir," I said when everyone had left.

"I thank'ee lad," he said.

"Were you there when... when it happened?"

"I was..." The old storyteller let out a long sigh. "Tis a fine sword," he gestured to my pack that sat atop Punter's back. "I take it you are apprenticed to some keeper of artifacts?" he asked.

"No, I... I want to be an adventurer! One day, I know we will have need of heroes again," I said.

"Can you give me any advice? If you were present at such a magnificent battle, I take it you were once a great warrior?"

"Lad… times have long since changed." The old man gently patted my shoulder. "You want my advice?"

I nodded.

"Take up a trade. Learn to farm, or make pottery – become a tanner for goodness' sake. Forget about adventure and heroism. That way of life has died, and those who chase it will find themselves very, very lost."

The storyteller patted my shoulder once more before he turned and walked away. I did not look up even once as I dragged myself toward the inn.

I left Punter in the stables with a fresh bundle of hay before I headed inside. I sat at a table sipping spicy cider and stared at my sword that lay before me. My mind drifted idly to the countless tales of heroism I'd heard in my lifetime. Sometimes I thought I'd give anything for the world to be like it used to.

"Oy! Look who it is. I say, it's little Quinn!"

I turned and saw a large boy walking toward me. Two others followed him. The large one I recognized, it was Melvin Crosk. The others seemed familiar, but I couldn't quite remember them.

"Quinn! 'ow you been lad?" Melvin slapped me on the back.

"Hi Melvin..." I said.

"Say, what's that in front of you?" he asked.

"You mean my sword?"

"Sword!? Ah Quinn, don't tell me you're still into all that adventure stuff!" A smile began to creep across Melvin's face. "Do you boys remember 'ow he used to dress up in his sackcloth tabard with that old stick?"

"Haha-ahaha!" One of Melvin's cronies guffawed.

My lips pursed as my bottom jaw stuck out.

"Ooh, phew." Melvin wiped a tear of laughter from his eyes. "Oh Quinn, you gotta let that stuff go my friend! It's time to grow up, be a man, y'know? That's what me an' the guys are here for. We're learning 'ow to become tradesmen." Melvin's chest swelled. "Anyway, how's that old granny of yours doing?"

"She... she passed away, two months ago," I said.

"Oh Quinn, I didn't mean ta... I'm sorry," Melvin said. "I mean, first your parents, an' now—"

"HEAR YE! HEAR YE!" A herald burst through the doors to the inn before Melvin could finish. "Great King Junip the Thirteenth has issued a decree! He calls the proud, the daring, to become a challenger, a knight, a champion of his royal order! If there are any so brave, you must seek him out in Castletown, and pray that you have what it takes!"

Sheer awe took hold of me. Never before had I heard of anything like this in my life. "Still think I should let that adventure stuff go?" I turned and asked Melvin with a smile.

"Ah Quinn, the new king is a kook! Haven't you heard? Look around, everyone is laughing!" Melvin said. "He's not looking for *real* adventurers. There is no adventure to be had anymore – you know that, Quinn."

I looked throughout the inn and Melvin was right, no one seemed to have taken the herald seriously. My stomach dropped for a moment, but only a moment. I didn't care what the others thought. Juniper had need of a champion, as I always knew it would.

I finished my cider and said goodbye to Melvin. In the morning, I would depart as early as possible and make my way to Castletown.

Chapter 3

On Hanging Day

It was days before I reached the heavy, iron gates of King Junip's red-stone castle. When we finally arrived, I dismounted and tied Punter to a hitching post. My knees wobbled, yet I was ready as ever to appear before this curious king. As I ascended to the gates of the inner castle, I was greeted by a herald.

"Hail, young lad!" He called out.

"Hail!" I responded vigorously.

"What brings you to the threshold of the King on this fine day?"

"I wish for an audience with the great one," I said. "I've heard that he may require assistance."

"Of course!" The herald raised a pointed finger. "The King won't be seeing anyone until his conference hours later this afternoon. But until then you can assist with Hanging Day!"

"Hanging Day?" I asked uneasily.

"But of course. It happens every time this year. Terrible work it is though," he said.

"Well, where does this event take place?"

"Right here in the castle."

"*In* the castle!?" I could scarcely believe.

"Where else would it be?" He asked.

"I don't know, some sort of courtyard or something?"

"Poppycock! That's the silliest thing I've ever heard. Go on then, it's just through those doors. Be quick about it!"

I stepped forward and placed a sweaty palm on the door, unsure if I wanted to see what lay beyond. Someone gasped as the cedar doors opened before me. Shielding my eyes, I heard the sound of metal clanging on a stone floor. I peeked through my cracked fingers and saw curtain rod bouncing to and fro.

"You clumsy fool!" An armor-clad knight jeered at a round, rosy-cheeked man. "If you drop one more item you'll be henceforth banned from all hanging days! D'ya hear?"

"Yes, sir! Forgive me, sir!" The round man quavered.

"Right then, back to it," said the knight.

Scanning the room, I saw people on ladders looking at the round man. When the knight moved on they all resumed working on various hanging projects! There were wall-flowers, paintings, curtains, and candle-sticks.

Phew! I thought. *This I can do!*

I began working immediately. A knight tasked me to remove old portraits from the wall, dust them thoroughly, then hang them again. It would have been an easy job if not for my dust allergy. The day passed and before I knew it the great inner room to the castle was completely dusted and furnished. The knight stepped forward from his post.

"Congratulations, citizens of Juniper!" He said. "This was perhaps the most successful Hanging Day I have ever witnessed!"

"Hooray!" The workers cheered.

"The King thanks you for your service. It is my privilege to invite you, on behalf of the King, to the after-party! Light refreshments will be served in Banquet Hall "C" until twilight. It's straight through those double doors, down the hallway and second door on your right."

The soon-to-be party-goers chattered quietly to each other with smiling faces as they departed. But I would not be joining them. I had an objective to complete, regardless of how much I enjoyed party mints and punch.

"Excuse me good sir," I said to the knight.

"Well met, citizen!" He stood to attention with an upright halberd.

"Well met!" I echoed. "I wish to—ta... ah... ACHOO!" My sneeze nearly lifted my feet from the ground.

"Oy!" The knight backed away and lowered his weapon. "Have you got the plague!?"

"No, sir! It's merely a dust allergy."

"Oh... right," he grinned sheepishly. "Well then, what can I do for you?"

"I wish for an audience with the King. I was told I may speak with him after participating in Hanging Day."

"But of course! He confers with the people 'round six o'clock, which is..." He looked over my shoulder and squinted at a sundial some ten feet away. "...in about two minutes. It's why I'm guarding these doors now," he said, gesturing to the doors behind him.

"Marvelous! May I enter?"

"Umm, no—nope. Sorry, the King is very particular about this sort of thing. You'll have to wait."

"Oh, um... alright." I moved to the side and sat on a cushioned bench. The knight immediately resumed his blank, forward stare. About two awkward minutes passed by and I pondered why no one else was waiting with me.

"Righto! On your feet you lot." The knight leaned his halberd toward me. "Conference hours have begun."

"Thanks..." I said. "Oh, before I enter. Is there a particular manner in which the King enjoys being addressed?"

"Mmm, nope, not really. Your highness, my lord, my liege, great King Junip... anything should do."

"Perfect, thank—"

"Oh wait!" The knight clapped an armored hand to his helmet. "DO NOT, under any circumstances, refer to him as *your majesty*."

"Haha!" I laughed, but quickly grew uncomfortable as the knight remained stoic. "Wait... are you serious?"

"Absolutely... Now move along, quickly if you like. In you go."

Chapter 4

GREAT KING JUNIP

I slid through the doors and entered a huge throne room cast in red light. Down rows of pillars I drifted, but as I neared the throne I noticed it was empty. Two knights stood guard on either side of the great chair.

A door on the wall behind them swung open and a short man entered. He carried such a horde of unusual objects that his face was hidden from view. Stumbling toward the throne, he released his burden in a pile. Only then did I see that he was also quite plump. His wide eyes, set beneath a gold crown, locked with mine.

"Oh!" he gasped. "Who are you!? What are you doing here?"

"Uh, f—forgive me sire. I did not mean to startle you," I stammered.

"Goodness! Is it time for my conference hours already?" He sat on his throne and mumbled to himself as he rubbed his knuckles. The King wore a purple robe under a red cape and his face was scruffy and unshaven. Black locks of his frazzled hair stuck out from under his crown in almost every direction.

"Alright then speak, speak!" He clapped his hands and a platter of broccoli was set before him by a servant I hadn't noticed. He chomped the tiny trees and stared straight into me.

Only slightly distracted by the odd snack, I began. "Ahem, yes, well..." I breathed deeply. This was it, the moment I had waited on for so long. My next words and the answer that followed would dictate the course of my existence. Drudgery and glory were to be cast as die in the great game of my life.

"Great King Junip..." I proceeded. "Mighty one of our land, I am before you today because... ah—ACHOO!" In an instant, my allergy betrayed me. I looked up at him, embarrassed and stunned. He returned a visage to me that was both grim and crazed. With a sweep of his hand the platter of broccoli flew into the air. Green bulbs were propelled in every direction as he dove into the pile of objects that lay beside the floor. I could only watch in dreadful awe.

He discarded items over his shoulder as he rummaged through his stock. A hat was flung to the left, a wooden wheel rolled to the right and a bag of marbles nearly hit me square in the chest. Then, he turned and unleashed the contents of a leather pouch directly at my face.

"Ach, ugh, ugh!" I coughed as the powdery substance floated through my nostrils and into my eyes. "ACHOO!" It only worsened the state of my tickling nose. I rubbed my face clean and saw the King standing before me expectantly.

"What did you do that for!?" I held my hands in the air and looked down – a blue powder stained my chest.

"Aha! It has remained blue!" The King threw his hands high and sighed. His shoulders relaxed and he sat back down on his throne.

Then he clapped his hands three times. "Attend to him!" He bellowed. From the corners of the room three servants with damp towels were upon me immediately. My jaw felt weighted to the floor and my hands were held out as if hoping for an explanation to fall from the sky.

Within seconds I was scrubbed clean.

"My apologies," said the King, "but one can't be too careful."

"Careful of what!?" I shrieked.

"Those who sneeze at first meetings may indeed harbor a Karfarfle in their spirit," he stated. "Had the powder turned red, we would have known there was a threat. Now then, where were we?"

"A Karfarfle?"

"Yes, a Karfarfle... nasty little creatures that I want nothing to do with. Now please, tell me why you are here."

"I'd heard you needed an adventurer," I said with annoyance. The magnitude of the moment was lost to absurdity.

He grasped the arms of his great chair and leaned forward. "You are here to answer the call!?"

"I... I am... I suppose."

"Huzzah!" He shouted. "Glorious!"

"Am... I the first to come?"

"Indeed you are! And just in time if you'd believe it! Oh wonderful day!" He jumped from his throne and rocked his hips while pointing his fingers in a terribly awkward celebration. Then he ran to my side and threw an arm around me. "My friend, you have the look of a hero about you! Has anyone ever told you that?"

"Well, uh—"

"Doesn't matter! I'm telling you now! I would be honored if you would be my champion!" He whistled sharply and a servant in puffy garments came forward bearing a scroll.

"By signing this contract you agree to four things. One, you will complete any quests I assign to you. Two, you will assemble a company to aid you in your quests. This group must contain an elf, a dwarf and a wizard. Three, you will reside here in my castle until the contract expires. Four, you must not eat garlic or onions and you must not drink coffee for the duration of the agreement." He shoved the scroll and a quill into my hands and grinned. "What do you say?"

"Uhh, I... well, I understand numbers one and three, but why must I quest with others? I'd prefer to go alone."

"Nonsense! There must be a group of adventurers and it must have an elf, a dwarf and a wizard. All great stories are made of that stuff. Don't you know that?"

"Well, okay I suppose. But what about number four? I happen to like coffee."

"Blugh!" he gagged and a pink tongue fell from his mouth. "Horrible stuff! It gives you ghastly breath and *that* is one thing I will NOT tolerate."

"Oh, well... alright then..." I stared at the parchment for a while then looked up at this zany king. He smiled broadly and widened his eyes.

I do suppose this is what I wanted... With an unsteady flick of the quill, I signed the parchment.

"Marvelous!" King Junip snatched the feathered pen and paper away from me and handed it to his servant who promptly rolled it up and carried it away. "Now then, let's get right to it! For your first mission, I have a very important question for you. Have you ever heard of *Summoner's Stratagem*?"

"Summoner's Stratagem..." I repeated. The name danced around elusively in my head as I searched for its root. "Wait... yes I think... no, do you mean the card game?"

"Aha! So you've heard of it! Oh wonderful lad! I knew I picked the right one for the job!" He jumped around and danced again before coming to a sudden halt. "Are you any good at it?" He asked, grabbing me by my shoulders.

"No. Well, at least I don't think so. I've never played it. But what has this got to do with—"

"Oh, woes!" The King fell to his knees. "Nine woes! Ten woes! You horrible, worthless boy!"

He gripped his hair as if to pull, then stopped abruptly. "Wait! The company, of course! Haha, I am a genius! You must go, go and find your companions." Suddenly his tone was sharp as a sword. "And make *sure* that one of them is good at it."

"Here," he said as he handed me a small chest. "This is the finest collection of cards in all of Juniper. Take it, find yourself the right companions and travel to Berrysboro for the annual tournament that begins in two weeks. Your quest is to *win me that trophy!*"

With chest in hand, my feet stayed planted and my heart fluttered. I looked at the knights as if to gain sympathy or some explanation, I'm not sure which. But they kept their professional, rigid demeanor and didn't acknowledge me. King Junip sat down in his throne.

"But I don't understand... if you have these great cards and if you know the game well enough, why don't you win the trophy for yourself?"

The King slouched in his seat. His head hung as low as the pendulum of a great, grandfather clock. "Alas..." he groaned, "I could wish for nothing greater. Ohhhhh..." he groaned. "I am, however, absolutely terrible at it." A tear rolled down his cheek.

"Oh, I... I'm sorry. I didn't mean to—"

"No, no! It's quite alright. I've come to terms with my shortcomings," the king blubbered. Then he sat bolt upright. "But I can assure you, I will not show the same grace to you. Time runs short! I suggest you leave. Go and find the right crew for the job! Win me that trophy!"

The King's knights hastily escorted me out of the throne room. Once outside I squinted and blinked, unaccustomed even to the orange light of dusk.

How the blazes am I supposed to find a wizard, a dwarf and an elf willing to join me!? I cursed my luck as I untied Punter and walked him into the village of Castletown, which was nestled at the foot of the King's estate. I needed a plan.

Chapter 5

COAXING A WIZARD

I went to speak to one who knew the lands better than I – one who could tell me where such peculiar partners could be found. After inquiring about the village map-maker and lore-keeper, I set off for his hovel just west of town. Inside, I was met by a kindly, gray-haired man in a simple, brown robe. As he listened intently to my plight, the corners of his mouth slowly drooped. I was soon to learn that my task was hopeless.

He told me of Dwelvon, a country located to the west of Juniper. There the Dwarves and the Elves lived together in harmony after the grand wedding of the Dwarf King Axer and the Elf Queen Leafilas. Then he told me of the Mage Tower that was the home to the wizards. It stood far to the southeast of Dwelvon. And finally he pointed to Berrysboro, which lay further north even than Castletown. My destinations couldn't have been further apart from one another, and it was impossible to ride the required distance before the tournament began.

The map, he gave to me as a gift. Generous as it was, it did little to ease my distress. Not two hours had passed since my task was assigned and already I had failed. Punter and I plodded towards the tavern where I could at least spend my somber night in relative comfort. He tickled my ear once or twice with a fuzzy snout. Sometimes my companion did seem to have a keen ability to read my feelings.

We stopped at a tavern called *The Northern Barrel*. It was a homely place with calm candlelight and the patrons were generally tranquil. I left Punter in the stables and paid for our lodgings. My empty coin-purse did nothing to help my condition. With the last of my money I purchased a pint of Ginger Ale and drank the warm liquid gladly. But when it was drained my fists thoughtlessly clenched and the desire to punch something stirred within me. As I sat, wallowing in the ugly face of my quandary, I was surprised by an unreasonably boisterous voice.

"Greetings, friend!" it said. I quickly lifted my head and saw a boy (maybe slightly older than me) standing before me in a gray robe with a heavy pack. His sandy brown hair fell past his eyes. "I say, do you mind if I join you? It seems the other tables are filled up."

"Be my guest..." I sighed.

"So, what brings you to Castletown?" THWUMP – his heavy pack fell to the floor of reeds.

"Well, I had hoped to become an adventurer for the King. But that dream has come to a grinding halt it seems." I smacked my dry lips.

"Oh... I see... how odd. I too, am mourning a dream tonight. I'm here to hand in my letter of resignation tomorrow." He sighed deeply and we sat staring at the table for a moment. "Well then, enough of that. You must be thirsty," he said, gesturing toward my empty stein. "Would you care for another drink?"

"It would be most welcome," I replied. My new friend waved his hand through the air. A white glow shined from his palm and my mug was miraculously filled with a deep purple beverage. I held my breath and stared with bright eyes at the delightful drink before me.

"It's Dewberry Nectar. I'm sure it's nothing compared to the innkeeper's Ginger Ale, but it does the trick," he said.

"What... *How did you do that!?*" I gasped.

He shrugged and said, "magic."

"You—You're a wizard!?"

"*Was* a wizard. As I said, I am here to quit. I am meeting with Archmage Fardron tomorrow to be stripped of my powers."

"What? Why would you do that?"

"It's not my choice," he said bluntly. "I've failed my test at the Mage Tower for the last time. The ceremony of my dispossession has been ordered by Grand Mistress Fredsel of the Tower. Tomorrow I will be a wizard no longer."

My brain was buzzing. *This was it! This was exactly what I needed! Well... Almost exactly what I needed.*

"My friend," I began, "what is your name?"

"Duncan," he said.

"Duncan! My name is Quinn, and I believe that we can help each other. The King has tasked me with a quest I thought impossible until now. I am to organize a team of a wizard, a dwarf and an elf, then travel to Berrysboro to compete in a tournament. I thought this was impossible because I could not travel to both the Mage Tower and Dwelvon within two weeks! But if you join me, we can do it!" I slapped an open palm on the table as glee took hold of me.

Duncan looked at me blankly before he shook his head. "You are misguided, friend. It's not up to me. The powers that be have commanded my fate. If I do not show up tomorrow, they will find me and force me to be decommissioned."

"But what if you were under the King's protection!? If you were a part of my company the King may order them to stand down."

Duncan's eyes widened only for a moment. "I... I don't know. Even if we do succeed, I'm not so sure the King could thwart the desires of both Archmage Fardron and Grand Mistress Fredsel. They're two of the most powerful people in all of Juniper."

"Duncan... I cannot guarantee that you will keep your magic, but what other choice do you have? There is a chance that the King can protect you, a good one at that! Don't give up on your dreams just yet... you don't want to spend your life wondering what might have happened, do you?"

I watched intently and time stood still as I observed his contemplation. His furrowed brow gave me little hope at first. But gradually he relaxed. He looked at me and his eyes were still.

His mouth was tight and his breathing, deep.

"Alright," he said.

"Alright you'll join me!?"

"I'll join you!" He slammed a fist on the table. "If there's a chance I'll get to keep my magic, then... then I want to take it."

I cheered heartily and clasped Duncan's arm. Overjoyed, we spent the rest of the night listening to the bard's telling of old adventures through story and song, each tale inspiring us more and more. When we awoke the next morning, only a little sleepy from being up too late, we quickly set off for the western region of Dwelvon.

Chapter 6

DWELVON

As Punter clopped along the dirt path, I turned and watched Duncan while he rode. He sat atop a mule named Molly and wore a great, pointy, straw hat to shade his eyes from the sun. Still, I could not believe that I rode alongside a wizard. It was more than I had hoped for.

We talked only a little as we travelled, but the nights spent by the fireside allowed us more time to learn about each other. Each night he would read from a great, leather-bound tome with ancient runes across the cover.

Duncan inevitably asked what kind of tournament we were attempting to win and I told him about the card game. I couldn't tell if he was surprised or relieved by the way he reacted. Unfortunately he didn't know anything about the game, so we'd have to find one in Dwelvon who did.

A few days passed and the landscape began to change. First the sandy mountains of Juniper leveled out and grasslands began to appear. Then the grasslands turned to forests of oaks and speckled pines. Finally the forests faded into scattered swamps with great palm trees towering above the quagmires. When we began to consistently see the palms I took our map out to study it more.

"Duncan..." I started, "Am I reading this wrong, or does this map indicate that Dwelvon is next to a great, coastal region?"

"Mmm..." Duncan stared at the parchment. "It does appear to be that way."

"Don't all the stories tell of the dwarves' great mountain fortresses and the elves living in enchanted woods?"

"Beats me," Duncan shrugged. "I never really made time for history lessons at the Mage Tower. I spent all my time practicing magic."

We continued down the road leading to Dwelvon and I wondered about the extent of

Duncan's magical abilities. He wasn't very keen to discuss his training in detail so I left it alone for now. As far as I was concerned, I desperately needed a wizard and Duncan's appearance was nothing short of a miracle. Besides, it was nice having someone who could produce food and drink from nothing. He showed me that he could also create biscuits and other breads as well as sparkling, spring water. But I had yet to see him do anything else with his mysterious power.

Soon we began to see dwarves and elves riding by. They would tip their hats or nod as they passed. By the end of the day an impressive outpost appeared as we carried on. The fort had walls that were made from ten-foot, palm tree trunks sharpened to a point. We rode to the gates under the skeptical gaze of two guards – one was a dwarf and the other an elf. They wore armor of thick palm bark lashed together to form wooden scales. Atop their heads sat steel skullcaps that oddly resembled halved coconuts.

"Halt!" Spat the dwarven guard as he stepped toward us. "What brings ye today to Fort Tortle, the Palm Gates of Dwelvon?"

"Uh, hello there," I replied. "We are just passing through and hoping to pick up a few recruits as we go."

"Recruits? What manner of recruits are you

hoping to find?" Asked the elf.

"Oy!" The dwarf exclaimed. "What're ye doin, Pierre? You know how this goes! I ask the questions, you make the declarations!"

"Oh not this again!" The elf rolled his eyes.

"Oh yes this again!" The dwarf walked to the other side of the gate and pushed a stumpy finger against the elf's chest. "I don't care how many times I have to say it, that's the way it is!"

"Well I think it's just ridiculous! I don't recall the captain assigning questioning duties! I think your head is just getting as fat as your belly..."

"Oh, ho! Is that so?"

"Yes, that's so! And I'll tell you another thing..."

Duncan leaned toward me. "What do we do?" He asked.

"I don't know, I suppose we should just go in." The dwarf now stood on his tip-toes so he could yell closer to the elf's face. We sidled through the gate without even a sideways glance from the guards.

We walked with our steeds until we were close to the town square. Once there, Duncan and I witnessed the most peculiar people bustling about the village. They were half elf, half dwarf! Some were six feet tall with four-foot, red beards and giant noses. Others were four feet tall with round bellies, slender faces and pointy ears. Still others included every variation of the described traits that you could possibly think of. Only a few of the citizens were pure elves and pure dwarves.

We began to ask the townsfolk if they knew of anywhere we could play *Summoner's Stratagem*. But the sun was quickly setting and most were not in a talking mood. We were brushed aside several times and others politely explained that they must be home for dinner. Just when we thought we'd have to give up, a stroke of luck guided us toward opportunity. A particularly short and round elf informed us that a group gathers to play every evening at a tavern called *The Portly Parrot.*

"They should begin playing in oh, say, a half-hour or so," he said with a curiously squeaky voice.

After locating the tavern, we made ourselves comfortable and waited for the festivities to begin. Only a few patrons drank quietly at the bar. The barkeep sat on a stool, idly polishing mugs and steins with a worn rag. An ancient and, well... portly, parrot sat on his shoulder with its eyes closed. Every now and then, a loud, squawkish snore escaped its beak.

A quarter of an hour passed before a group

of patrons arrived and quickly pushed several tables together. Most of them appeared to be very young, but there were two or three who looked to be forty years of age. They ordered some refreshments from the innkeeper and all began organizing decks of cards. This was the bunch we were looking for.

We watched at a distance for a while and gained more understanding of the game, but mostly it still remained a mystery to me. I decided to introduce myself and watch more closely. As soon as I stood the door to the inn swung open again. All of the players looked up for a moment. When they saw the dwarf at the door they grumbled together before resuming play.

This new arrival entered with his chin held high and some sort of carrying case in his right hand. He looked exceptionally young – I guessed him to be no older than 11 or 12. He had a thin, red beard that was longest at his chin. A green felt cap sat on his head and came to a point at the front. He also wore round-framed glasses and his face had far less wrinkles than any of the dwarves I'd seen that day.

He strode to a nearby table, opened his case and began organizing decks of cards. When he finished, he took a book out and casually flipped through the pages.

Though I was curious about him, I decided to remain on course and get more information from the group. As Duncan and I approached, they gladly permitted us to sit nearby and were more than happy to answer any questions we could come up with. Eventually, I asked about the dwarf who still made no effort to participate.

"Borzun," someone said his name. "He comes every night and sits there, waiting to be challenged."

"Is he any good?" I asked.

"The best," they replied. "We'd really like him if he wasn't such a pompous prune."

Now my interest piqued. This was potentially the dwarf I needed. I didn't care if he was agreeable or not, I only cared that he could win. As we talked, a bearded elf sitting on the far side of the tables got up and approached Borzun. The elf sat. Borzun set his book down and rubbed his hands together.

"First victim!" He shouted with a smug smile. The elf did not seem amused. As they began the game I could see that Borzun was quickly gaining the advantage. Minutes later, the elf grimaced as Borzun made the final play with a patronizing comment. His opponent gathered his cards with a frown and returned to the group.

Throughout the night I learned much and even played a few games with random cards I grabbed from the King's chest. Many times I saw challengers approach Borzun, but always they left in defeat.

When I won my first game against a young, dwarven player, many of my new friends congratulated me. Pleased with my victory and feeling a little reckless, I decided it was time to meet Borzun.

Chapter 7

LAYING DOWN THE GAUNTLET

I left Duncan while I went to speak with our potential recruit. Duncan had forged his own deck and was rather into the game at this point, though he didn't seem to be very good at it.

"Hey there!" I sat at the table with my chest of cards. Borzun closed his book and looked up at me with a wry smile.

"Oh, I haven't seen you here before. Fresh meat! I like it!"

I recoiled slightly at his remarks, but said nothing for now. He took out more decks of cards and began sorting through them.

"So," he said, "how long have you been playing S.S.?"

"S.S.?" I asked.

He paused and looked up at me with a chuckle. "*Summoner's Stratagem*... duh!"

"Oh, well, this is my first time I suppose. But actually I was hoping we could talk first. You see—"

"Whoa, whoa, whoa!" He grinned and held both of his hands in the air. "*This is your first time*? Please... stop wasting my time and go sit back down at the kids table."

My frown twisted to a grimace as he picked his book up and seemingly gave me no more thought. Some choice words came to mind in the moment, but I collected myself and decided to take a more tactful approach. If he really was as good as they said, then I couldn't afford to let this opportunity slip.

"Well..." I said, "I can understand that. I'd sure hate to lose to a first time player were I in your position."

"What?" He shut his book and stared at me.

"Well I'm just saying... I understand how that would be too big of a risk for you to take. I mean, you'd probably win, but if you didn't win you'd be devastated. I'll go back and tell the guys you declined to play because there was too much at stake."

"No, no, no... I declined to play because you're not worth my time. I'll only play if I know it's going to be at least some sort of challenge."

"Hmm," I shrugged my shoulders and started to walk away. "Well that seems convenient."

"Wait! What did you say?"

"I said it seems convenient. I guess it's easy to be undefeated if you're that selective about who you play. Maybe you're not as good as they say you are..."

"Alright, that does it!" He yelled. I watched as the entire group of players paused and looked at us. "Get back here! If you want to play, I'll play. I was trying to be nice. I was trying not to hurt your feelings. But if that's how you're gonna be then I'll be glad to teach you a lesson!"

I sat back down at the table with Borzun, satisfied that I had at least won the first battle. As I opened the chest containing the King's cards, for the first time I noticed a small pocket in the silk lining. From the pocket, I removed a bound deck of cards that had already been assembled. After I unwrapped the binding I thumbed through them slowly and smiled. These cards were good – the King must have had some help in assembling this deck.

"Alright," said Borzun. "Since you're so

confident, I'll let you go first." The look on his face reminded me of a viper ready to strike. Perhaps I had riled him a little too much…

"Splendid," I gulped. I set my deck down and drew my first cards. As I looked at my hand, I thought mostly about how I was going to convince him to join me. My foot was in the door, but my concern was that his foot would soon be kicking my rear.

As we played, it became clear that my cards were far better than Borzun's. But he still managed to deal with every one of my threats. I could tell that his interest in my collection was growing as we continued on. Toward the end of the game, a crowd of onlookers had gathered. The match was growing close enough to make Borzun perspire. I drew a card and it seemed good, so I played it without much thought. Borzun stopped and stared with a stone face and the audience gasped as they saw it.

"Is… Is that Zebe the Giant, Epic, Dragon-slayer?" Borzun whispered.

I glanced at the card and fumbled for a reply. "Uh, well—ehrm, I mean—Yes, yes it is. Of course it is."

Borzun still spoke in a quiet monotone. "That card was featured in The Card Geek Gazette three times. There were only 4 copies ever made..." Then he rubbed his eyes and began searching through his hand for a response. Beads of sweat dripped from his great, dwarven nose and he struggled to keep his glasses from sliding off his face.

Two turns later, he had destroyed my card and we both stood on the edge of defeat. I searched through my hand for anything that would win me the game, but found nothing. I was forced to make a defensive play and hope for the best. When Borzun saw my move, he let out a sigh of relief and bested me with his final play.

The crowd erupted chaotically. Most groaned, but others cheered while some still stood in silence with wide eyes. Borzun leaned back in his chair and smiled at the ceiling as the group dispersed. Some went back to the tables to play and others left the inn for the night, but I gathered my cards and remained seated.

"Very well played, my friend. That was impressive," I said.

"Thank you!" He replied. "And you—well, *where did you get those cards!?*"

"I've recently inherited them."

"Inherited?"

"That's right. They were given to me... *by the King of Juniper.*"

"You can't be serious." He looked at me in

disbelief.

"I am serious. And if you're interested I may consider giving some of them to you. That is, *if* you will help me with something."

"Name your price!" His response was immediate.

"Good, I'm glad you said so. Do you see that man over there?" I asked, pointing to Duncan.

"The stumble-bum in the straw hat?"

"That's the one. He's a wizard, actually, and he and I are on a mission. We are questing for the King of Juniper, and right now the King wants us to win the annual Summoner's Stratagem tournament in Berrysboro."

"You mean the Berrysboro Brawl!?" Borzun shouted through grinning teeth. He brought both of his hands up and rested them on top of his head.

"I've not heard it called that, but I suppose so."

"Yes!"

I raised an eyebrow inquisitively. "You mean..."

"I want to come, especially if I can use those cards. Can we leave tonight?" He asked.

"Well hold on now, I appreciate the enthusiasm but we've still got to find an elf to join us before we leave."

"Perfect. My brother is an elf. Well, he's my half-brother, but he'll want to come too."

"How old is your brother?" I asked skeptically.

"He's 16 years old."

"And he'll want to leave tonight too? Shouldn't we wait until the morning to ask him?

"No!" Borzun shouted as he gripped the table. I was taken aback by the force of his emotion. "If you want us to come, we must leave tonight."

Chapter 8

MIDNIGHT FLIGHT

I pondered the situation carefully, unsure of exactly why Borzun wanted to leave so quickly. But after a moment or two I decided this was the best chance we had. Whatever was to come of it, here was a player who could win the tournament – *and* he could bring an elf.

"Okay..." I finally said. "We leave tonight *if* you can convince your brother to come with us."

"That'll be no problem. Come on, let's get moving." Borzun hastily gathered his cards and put them back in his carrying case. I did the same and called Duncan to join us.

"Hold on chum!" Duncan hollered. "Let me finish this game here."

Borzun walked up to him and looked at the cards that were on the table. He moved behind Duncan's opponent and studied his hand. Then he swiftly took two cards from the hand, despite slight opposition from the player, and played a maneuver that totally defeated Duncan.

"There," Borzun said. "Game's over, butter-fingers. Now let's go."

Duncan looked at me, his bottom jaw stuck out and he snorted once. I shrugged at him and packed my things before we left. In the dark of night we stole away to Borzun's home. Soon we came to a stone wall that stood around a grand estate.

"Wait here," said Borzun. Then he climbed a specific section of the wall with practiced skill. Duncan and I looked at each other uneasily as we sat upon our steeds and waited in the blackness. Our animal companions seemed to share in our concerns. Punter began pawing at the dirt and Molly started to whimper.

A clamor broke the silence from the other side of the wall and was quickly followed by a loud crash. I could barely breathe past the knot of stress forming in my chest, and that was *before* I heard the hounds barking. Fortunately, we didn't have to wait much longer. I heard Borzun's voice from the other side of the wall – he seemed to be arguing. Then he screamed and I saw him flying over the stone structure. He flailed awkwardly with a quarterstaff in one hand and a satchel slung over his arm. His shoulder smashed into the ground and he rolled ungracefully. Gasping for air and winded from his tumble, he fumbled to put his glasses back on his nose.

Then a gigantic figure, both tall and wide, bounded to the top of the wall and jumped down. The earth trembled slightly at his landing. I tried to move toward Borzun to help him up, but Punter was spooked by the looming giant. I fought for control of my horse and saw Duncan having a similar struggle with Molly. Then the great silhouette ran to Borzun and picked the dwarf up. He walked toward me with Borzun in his arms and within his shadowy frame I saw huge, pointy ears.

He's an elf! Truly, he was the biggest elf I had ever seen, not that I had seen too many before.

"Can he ride with you?" The elf asked in a startlingly deep voice.

"Yes, yes!" I shouted. The hounds' alarm was just on the other side of the wall now.

The elf sat Borzun on the saddle behind me.

"How will you keep up?" I asked as he secured Borzun.

"I'll keep up," he said gruffly.

"Punter, fly!" I shouted as I felt Borzun grip my torso. We dashed toward the city exit and I heard the gate to the estate open. Angry bellowing from a small host of men erupted under the shrill screams of an unknown taskmaster.

Something whizzed over my head and thudded into the wall of a palm tree house. "Are they shooting at us!?" I yelled.

"Just go!" Borzun shouted back. Stones and arrows continued to sing around us.

As we passed through the city gates I heard the guards shout something like "Hey, stop!"

But they were in no position to chase us down at the pace we were going. Once we were at a safe distance from the outpost, we slowed to a trot but continued to travel all night. I had no intention of letting our pursuers catch us asleep on the side of the road.

I asked Borzun who they were, but he just grumbled sleepily. "Talk in the morning," he said. We rode for hours under a starry sky. Finally, just before dawn broke the deep blue horizon, we stepped off the road and collapsed in the first flat clearing we could find.

Chapter 9

Raising the Stakes

We woke around noon and I introduced myself to our newest companion. In the light of day I saw that he was, as I had supposed from the shadows, an elf.

"Hello there, I'm Quinn and this is Duncan."

"Olivander," he said as he gripped my forearm with a huge hand.

"So, Borzun tells me you're his brother," I said.

"Aye, 'tis true," said Olivander. Borzun approached after hearing his name.

"Can either of you explain who was chasing us with stones and arrows last night?" Duncan asked with a hint of annoyance.

Borzun and Olivander exchanged glances. Borzun appeared slyly satisfied and Olivander looked as though he was ready to crush something.

"Friends," said Borzun, "you've just helped us to escape from one of the most ruthless men in all of Dwelvon."

"Oh…" Duncan sighed and shook his head.

"Who might that be?" I asked. "And do tell why we needed to flee from him like that in the dead of night."

"Baron Bulgar. He's an evil man that one is," said Olivander.

Borzun sat down and took a swig from a waterskin. "Well, last year Olivander and I lost our parents in an accident." I thought I saw a tear come to Olivander's eyes as Borzun spoke.

"So," Borzun continued, "after that, we were forced to go out on our own and look for work. Baron Bulgar offered us jobs tending to his estate and told us that we could even live on his grounds. Without any other options, we signed his labor contract and were living there for about five months or so. During that time we saw the true nature of the Baron, he's a cruel man and he never ceased to deal harshly with us. So, we decided to leave."

"But when we told him," Olivander growled, "he pulled out our labor contract and showed us a few pieces of fine print that we had overlooked. We owed him a heap of money for our rent and meals. He told us that if we left without paying him, he'd have us thrown in prison until our debt was paid."

Borzun clenched his fists until his knuckles were white. Then he continued. "Olivander and I started saving every copper piece to pay our debt. Two weeks ago we brought our sum to the Baron and he laughed at us. He took our money then showed us that we were more in debt now than we were before."

"That's terrible!" I exclaimed.

"We talked about fleeing," Olivander grumbled. "But we heard stories from the other laborers. Always when people left without paying their debts, they were chased down and tossed in jail by Bulgar's thugs."

"But when you two came along," said Borzun, "a wizard and a champion of the King, I knew it was the chance we had been waiting for!"

Duncan and I looked at each other uneasily.

"D-do you think he'll come for us?" Duncan

stammered.

"Almost certainly," said Olivander.

"And when they do come, you'll zap them all with lighting, won't you Mr. wizard!? And you, champion, the King won't hesitate to send troops to your aid, will he!?" Borzun asked joyfully.

"Well... Borzun, you really should have told us about this," I said.

"Borzun... they look much younger than you made them seem, what exactly made you think they could protect us?" Olivander asked.

I held my breath and puffed once through my nostrils as Olivander spoke. Then I put my face in my hands... *He was right.*

"Let's make it to Berrysboro and win that tournament first," I finally said. "If we can please King Junip with our victory we very well may have all the protection we'll need."

The conversation ended somewhat tensely. Borzun and Olivander seemed rather anxious when they realized that we may not be the great defenders they were looking for. And Duncan and I were now dealing with the suspense of travelling with wanted men. Duncan was already a wanted man himself, of course, but he only faced the threat of losing his powers. Based on what Borzun had shared, there was no telling what our new pursuers would do to us if we were caught.

It seemed the stakes of this card game had been raised yet again. All our hopes were resting on our worth to King Junip. There was no question about it anymore... we just *had* to win that trophy.

Chapter 10

An Unfortunate Meeting

After nine days of travel I began to grow tired of Duncan's conjured breads. They were extremely convenient and they didn't taste bad, but it just wasn't the same as a loaf straight out of the oven. It was always cold and it felt like it had been sitting out for about three days.

That night Olvander and I went hunting together with his short bow. It was quite a sight to watch him wield it, for it looked like a toy when he held it in his great arms. After we had killed a deer and packed the meat, we began the trek back to our campsite. My curiosity got the better of me and I decided to strike up a conversation.

"So, Olivander," I said. "Do you mind if I ask you a personal question?"

"It won't bother me," he replied.

"Well, you're half dwarf and half elf, right?"

"No, I'm just an elf. Why do you ask?"

"Oh... well, it's just that Borzun said you were his half-brother."

"That's just what he says. Truly we're step-brothers, but we've been through so much together, Borzun and I. We may not share blood, but it makes us no less brothers than anyone else."

When we got back to the camp I prepared our dinner and we all feasted on wild venison roasted over the fire – all of us, except for Olivander that is. Instead he foraged for some garden vegetables and made a salad. I found it curious, but made no effort to talk about it.

The next day we traveled as fast as we could. The tournament was only four days away and we'd have to make good time to be sure we got there early enough to register.

Our evenings seemed to pass quickly while the days grew long under the oppressive glare of the sun. But soon enough, in the sandy landscape of Juniper, the village of Berrysboro appeared over the horizon.

In the village the townspeople were bustling with energy. We asked where we could find the registration table for the tournament and they directed us to the town square. On our way there we passed an enormous hole in the ground with a plank that extended over the vast pit.

"What do you think that's for?" Duncan asked.

"Ah don't worry about it, it's not important," said Borzun.

"That's right," I added. "Right now we just need to be focused on winning this game."

Soon we found the table at the town's center. There was a line of participants stretching back about 100 paces, so we joined in at the rear. From the look of things, it seemed like we'd be waiting for a while.

We were halfway through when I heard the most terrible, horrible noise. It was a cavalier, conceited and condescending voice. The bitter sound, like the head of a shovel striking stone, dug up intense feelings of hatred from my childhood.

"Well, well, well… if it isn't little Quinn!" Said the voice. I turned around and confirmed my feelings of disgust. There he stood, garbed in fine chainmail armor with a golden plate pauldron.

He was about two years older than me and his perfectly wavy, blonde hair was tucked behind a perfectly polished, silver circlet.

Next to him stood a beautiful girl with black hair wearing a dazzling silver and deep-blue robe. In her hand she held a staff crested with a scarlet sapphire. Behind both of them there was a lean elf-man in beautifully crafted leather armor and a forest green cape. Finally, next to the elf was a dwarf with a thick, braided beard. He was wearing heavy iron armor and he had a great axe slung over his back.

"Caden," I said. "What are you doing here?"

The girl stepped forward with a wry smile. "Quinn, aren't you going to say hello to me? I'm hurt... it's as if you don't recognize me."

I squinted and strained my memory. "Aila?" I said hesitantly.

"That's right!" She laughed. "It's okay, I almost didn't recognize you without your stick and your tabletop!" Caden joined in her laughter and my companions all looked at me curiously.

"What are you doing here?" I repeated.

"Well we're here to win the tournament!" Caden said. "We've been enlisted by King Junip to win the trophy." My stomach churned as Caden continued. "I was worried when he said he'd already recruited his champion, but I should have known I could sway him! Talent like this doesn't exist anymore. Aila and I put on a show for him and he couldn't refuse us! It's only too bad that he gave his cards away to the first set of adventurers he met. I'll wager we may see them..." Caden slowly stopped talking and began sizing up the rest of my troupe.

"Wait just a minute..." A broad grin appeared his face. "Are they with you?" He asked as he gestured toward Duncan, Borzun and Olivander.

"They are," I replied.

"Haha! Oh dearie, don't tell me... You're the adventurers!? Oh this is too good!" Caden chuckled. "Where did you even find this lot? They look as poor and dejected as you!"

"Poor and dejected!?" Borzun shouted. "We'll see who's looking dejected after I've finished mopping the floor with that golden, pretty-boy hair of yours."

"Watch your mouth, dwarfling!" Caden step-ped forward and towered over Borzun. As he did, Olivander moved behind Borzun and Caden became lost in his shadow.

"I would take a step back if I were you..." Olivander growled. Aila's hand began to glow white and she stood ready. The elf behind them removed a bow from his shoulder strap while the dwarf cracked his knuckles.

Caden looked up at Olivander with a grimace and reluctantly took a step back. "And what are you supposed to be?" Caden spat. "Some kind of elf-ogre come to save your pet dwarf?"

Olivander began to advance but I jumped in front of him just in time. "Enough of this!" I yelled. "We are here for the tournament, not to waste time bickering with the likes of you. Please, leave us be and take your place at the end of the line."

"Aww," Aila smiled, "he's begging you, Caden."

Caden smiled back at her. "Since he asked nicely, I suppose we can leave it alone today. But Quinn, true heroes don't wait in line. I hope you're ready to lose your good graces with the King – you should be familiar with that right? Losing?" Caden grinned. "Losing is one thing you always were good at. We'll see you at the games!" He turned and the others followed his lead.

"Oh and Quinn," he shouted back, "you should bring your sackcloth tunic! You know, for old times' sake!"

They all laughed as they walked directly up to the table and placed a small bag of coins in front of the attendants. The workers quickly pocketed the bag and allowed Caden and his friends to enter immediately. I looked at Duncan, who had been speechless the whole time. He was trembling slightly.

"Who were those bramble-pants?" Borzun grunted.

"No one," I replied. "They're nothing but unpleasant memories from my childhood. Let's just get registered and find a bed for the night."

In another half hour Borzun was signed in, so we headed to the nearest inn and purchased a room for the night. Then we tried to get some sleep as we anxiously waited for dawn to bring forth the day of the tournament.

When morning came I sat up in my crude cot and rubbed the sleep away from my eyes. I looked across the room and saw Borzun asleep on the top bunk – his face was smashed into the mattress and his rump stuck straight in the air, rising and falling with every snoring breath. Olivander slept beneath him on the bottom bunk in perfect silence with his hands clasped on his chest.

I yawned and walked to the window. Light filled the room when I opened the shutters.

"Ohhh, errrm, five more minutes..." Borzun mumbled. He covered his head with his pillow.

"Oh come now!" I snorted. "It's the day of the tournament! We've gotta be ready, we've gotta be limber, we've gotta be spry!"

"Bluuugghhh…" Duncan rolled over onto his face.

"Well come on…" I said. "We've at least got to be awake…"

Chapter 11

THE BERRYSBORO BRAWL

With some more coaxing I eventually got everyone out of bed and we headed downstairs for breakfast. The innkeeper served us a bland porridge with a hunk of buttered bread. We ate quickly and thanked him for the meal. Eagerly, we left to see the tournament grounds that were being set up outside. After our first look at the preparation of the games, not one of us was unimpressed. A great, multicolored tent had been erected and hundreds of tables were setup underneath it.

Tournament officials wearing bright-yellow

tunics were rushing around making final adjustments. Far to the north and west of the tent, two grand, makeshift arenas now stood where nothing had been on the night before.

The grounds were absolutely buzzing with activity. Players and spectators alike were reviewing schedules and making predictions for the tournament ladder. Vendors and merchants drifted through the crowd pushing carts filled with various delicacies. I spotted roasted rabbits on a stick, strawberry cream tarts the size of my head, dollops of delicious, cinnamon-almond pudding, candied chestnuts, turkey legs, sizzling bacon and keg after keg of perfectly frothy beverages.

Drifting aimlessly among the sea of spectators and peddlers, we quickly lost track of time. Soon trumpets blew that summoned the players for their first-round games. I smacked my head with the palm of my hand when I heard them.

"Borzun!" I said, "We'll be late! Quickly, run back to the room and grab your cards. I'll try to stall the officials."

Borzun just looked at me with a stoic expression. "I've got everything I need right here." He patted his satchel that hung by his side.

I smiled and breathed easily. My confidence

in Borzun reached a new height. But my faith was tested quickly. His first match was against a man who was easily qualified to be a contender in the finals. With a little luck Borzun was barely able to defeat him.

The next few games were not quite so challenging and the rest of the day quickly passed without incident. I noticed that with each game we won, the next became more crowded with rowdy fans. Groups of onlookers began to form around players they had chosen as their favorite. Borzun's following had become fairly large after his 15-game win-streak that he ended the day on.

"Well it looks like your spot for the semifinal match tomorrow is secured," said Duncan as we viewed the tournament ladder board.

Borzun said nothing, but slowly smiled.

"Isn't that your... *friend*, Quinn?" Olivander pointed at a name high up on the ladder seating.

"Aila..." I said with a sigh.

"It looks like she's playing for her spot in the semifinal now," Duncan added.

"We should watch," said Borzun. "I'd like to see how she plays."

With a quick turn, we started toward the tent where Aila's match was ongoing. When we arrived, the game looked as though it had just begun. The fans were cheering wildly with every decisive play, but we watched in silence. Not a muscle moved in Borzun's broad face as he studied the contest.

The match quickly progressed and Aila seemed to be winning. The spectators let out a spirited applause as she played the final card to ensure her position in the semifinal. We turned and left, still not speaking.

"She's good," Borzun finally said when we arrived at the inn.

"You can beat her, little brother," Olivander assured him as he slugged his sibling on the shoulder.

"We shouldn't be surprised... she is a wizardess, after all," said Duncan. "We spell casters are known for our superior intellect." The rest of us hid our faces and looked toward one another with quizzical humor.

"Well," continued Duncan. "I'm going down to the tavern for a drink. We should celebrate Borzun's success!"

"No, no," said Borzun. "I think I'd better stay here and work on my strategies for tomorrow.

"I think Duncan may be right," I attempted to persuade Borzun. "You did well today, now you need to relax a little or you'll wear yourself out before tomorrow comes."

Olivander agreed and Borzun reluctantly complied. The Inn's barkeep served us his specialty – sweet-spiced-ginger green tea with cinnamon-honey scones. We devoured them as the tavern bard regaled us with highlights of the day's games. Each time he mentioned one of Borzun's victories we all cheered as loud as we could and patted him on the back vigorously. But before long the moon began to fall and we realized we needed to get some sleep.

The following morning we awoke to an anxious quiet. Unlike the previous day, Borzun was the first to rise and he sat staring out the sunny window in silence until the rest of us were ready. We made our way to the schedule board and saw that his semifinal was to be played within the hour. Borzun's face grew pale.

"I didn't know it would be so soon…" he said.

"Come on, brother." Olivander threw a great arm around him and headed back toward the inn. "Let's get some breakfast."

Chapter 12

BETTER FORTUNES

Once at the inn we were quickly seated and our food was set before us.

"So," said Duncan through a mouthful of bread, "what tactics will you use to win this match!? Will it be heavy defense or heavy offense? Oooh ooh, will you use a good bit of trickery or do you think brute force will be the key!?

Borzun stared at his plate and poked a lump of cheese with his fork.

"I say, chap, did you hear me?" Duncan questioned. "I said, are you going to—Ow!"

Duncan yelped as I kicked him under the table.

"Leave it alone, Duncan," I said through clenched teeth.

The rest of our meal was held with only brief moments of awkward small talk. Borzun ate nothing and said nothing, though his face had more color by end of it. We picked up our plates and brought them to the barkeep before we headed toward the arena.

Long before the stadium came into view, the deep, rumbling roar of thousands of voices filled our ears. When we made it to the gates, the noise was overwhelming. Borzun was led through an entrance on the ground level while we were directed to travel upwards into the stadium.

But the crowd of spectators waiting to enter was huge. We shuffled through the herd with little ease until our progress came to a sudden halt. After remaining at a standstill for nearly ten minutes, the match was coming dangerously close to starting and we were nowhere close to taking our seats.

"This is outrageous!" I shouted. "I'm going to look for another way in."

"Don't be silly," said Olivander. "By the time you find another way, the game will be over."

"Well we're not making any progress here!" I left the scene and pushed my way through those behind us. Running down rows of ramps to the bottom of the arena, I frantically searched for another way. My eyes were led to a dark corridor that ran beneath the stands. I could tell that there was some sort of light shining from the other side, so I set out to find where the tunnel might end.

Rushing into the darkness, I soon found that the light became eerily green. The source seemed to be just out of view beyond some sort of turn in the path. Though the tunnel was deceptively long, I could tell the light was getting closer and closer with every step.

As I neared the corner where the light was shining, I saw a hunched figure leaning against the wall. Once I was even closer, I could barely make out the form of an old woman in a cloak. She seemed to be mumbling to herself quietly. I glanced at her, then quickened my pace and continued toward the light.

"Hello, Quinn," she croaked.

"Excuse me?" I halted. I could feel my heart thrumming in my chest.

"I said hello, Quinn. Usually it's customary to say hello in return," she smiled.

"How... Have we met before?"

"In a way, we have. You don't know much about me, but I know all about you... Quinn

Alvaret." The woman removed her hood exposing silver hair and leathery, yet smooth, skin.

"Oookay... Ahem, well... I should be going then, I need to see the match that's about to begin. It was nice meeting you," I said.

"Meeting me?" She scoffed. "You haven't even cared to learn my name but you say it was nice meeting me?"

"Yes, well, begging your pardon miss. I do have to be going."

"Quinn... you spent so much of your life searching for your destiny. Why now do you run from it?"

"Run from it? Uh... what on earth are you talking about?"

"You're here to see me, you just didn't know it." She took a step closer. "Give me your hand. I'll show you what you came for."

I gulped. Something about this woman made me quite uncomfortable. But not in a way that felt dangerous. It was more like when my great aunt Olga came to visit.

Her face seemed kindly and there was no evil in her features. My curiosity was stronger than the churning feeling in my stomach, so I reached out a hand and clasped hers.

As soon as we touched a vision overcame

me. The rushing sensation felt like I had been catapulted through the air and was tumbling around and around. Then I saw a great volcano with ash rising into the sky. I saw fire and magic, ice and wind. I saw... wait... is that a?... I saw a giant red turtle...

Then there was Duncan, sitting alone in a swamp-hut. I saw the land of Juniper, desolate and charred. A looming presence entered. A roaring dragon flashed its wings and a cloaked figure stood silently amidst burning flames.

"You, Quinn, are destined for unrivalled adventure," came the woman's tired voice. "With all the joys and pains that accompany it, you will find what you seek. Now, go and see that the day is yours."

As her words faded the rushing sensation stopped. I opened my eyes but no light came to them. Total darkness shrouded me.

"What did you do? Where are we!?" I shouted at the woman, but no answer came. "Hello?"

I sat still to let my eyes adjust and slowly I began to see dark shapes. As my vision returned, I realized that I was still in the same passageway, only there was no green light and the roaring of the spectators had completely disappeared.

I started down the pathway toward the

entrance to the man-made tunnel. An orange light grew stronger as I walked.

Oh, great... I thought. I'd had just about enough of strange colored lights that day. But as I got closer I saw that this light was natural... It was a sunset.

Sunset? But Borzun's match took place in the morning... What did she do to me?

Still I heard no one, but as I emerged from the pathway I saw an old man sweeping garbage into a barrel.

"Excuse me, sir. Have you got the time?" I asked.

"Aye, it be nigh seven o'clock in the evening, it be," he said.

Seven o'clock...The grand final was supposed to begin at 6:30!

Faintly, I heard a sound like an "Ohhhhhh!" immediately followed by "Ahhhhh!" It was the sound of several thousand entertained on-lookers. Across the town stood the other arena, filled with noises of fantasy-battle, and I rushed toward them with all my strength.

"Blast it!" I shouted as I arrived. The same predicament I faced this morning crushed my aspirations of seeing the match. Every ramp I could see was packed with hopeful peasants, trying to get to a spot where they could see. A field mouse sat by my boot, nibbling on a scrap of bread.

"Urrrrgh!" I swung a kick at him, but he scurried away with ease. The mouse stopped three feet away, turned, sat upright on his haunches and stared at me with wiggling whiskers. As I looked into his beady, little eyes I was overcome with guilt.

"I'm sorry little guy..." I bent down to pick up the scrap of bread and tossed it to him. He immediately began nibbling again.

"Quinn! I say, Quinn old chap! Boy, you're not what I expected to find coming back from the latrine." Duncan's eager voice could not be mistaken.

"Duncan! It's you! What happened!? Did Borzun win his semi-final?"

"Of course he did! I say, *what happened to you!?* We've been looking all over to find you!"

"I know... I'm sorry... I don't know what... Duncan, have you ever met a true prophetess?"

Duncan's eyes widened. "A prophetess!? Quinn, if anyone ever claims to be one, you stay away, d'ya hear? Nothing but trouble those prophets are. What did she tell you?"

"Well, she said—"

"Ohhhhh!" The roar of the audience echoed.

"Duncan, we'd better do this later, do you

have a place for me to sit?"

"Of course! We've been allowed to sit on the field with Borzun. Come on, I'll show you!"

Duncan led me to a gate where a he showed the guard a carved, green block. He let us in and we hurried up a narrow ramp onto the pitch of the arena. There were three chairs set up about ten feet away from a grand table where Borzun sat. Olivander already occupied one of the seats where Duncan and I soon joined him.

"Quinn!" Olivander shouted over the noise and clasped my arm. "Where have you been!?"

"I'll have to explain later!" I turned toward the battle-table and saw Borzun lay down a card.

"YAAAAHHHHH!!!" The crowd let loose a crazed howl.

Aila's features were grim, but she took a deep breath and refocused. Meticulously, she searched through her hand, rearranging cards and silently calculating. A smile crept across her face as she played all four of her cards in a very specific order. They remained face down.

"By Fardron's fedora!" Duncan gasped. "She's played four mystery cards! Ohhh, this could be bad..." Duncan began chewing on his nails.

Borzun laughed. It was not his usual mocking laugh, nor was it an expression of joy.

He laughed relief, and looked toward us where we observed. Smiling broadly, he turned back toward Aila and played a single card.

"OHHHH MYYY!" An official shouted through a magical cone that amplified his voice. "WHO COULD HAVE PREDICTED THIS!? BORZUN HAS PLAYED... *WARLOCK HOLMES!*" The crowd exploded with such ruckus that I thought the stands would collapse all around us.

Aila bit her lip and, slowly, she gathered all the cards she had just played and tossed them into the discard pile. Then she drew a card and stared at it. With a gulp, she tossed it into the discard pile as well. Then, grabbing a white handkerchief that was draped over her side of the table, she flung it to Borzun.

An official on Borzun's side of the table raised a red flag in each hand, and the audience erupted into chaos.

"AILA SUBMITS! AILA SUBMITS!" The official with the magical cone shouted. Again, the stadium shook under the stampeding crowd. I could barely hear myself speaking over the outcry.

"Olivander! Did he win?" I shouted.

"Aye!" Olivander roared with a smile. "He won!"

Chapter 13

FROM GLORY TO BEEHTWULS

In no time at all, a makeshift stage was constructed in the arena. We were hurried to the top of the platform as the spectators filled the stadium. Borzun was ecstatic as we stood together on stage.

"Quinn, you made it!" He said. "Thank you, Quinn, thank you. If you hadn't come to Dwelvon I... well I don't even want to think about where I'd be!"

I smiled and nodded in reply. "I'm glad you

came, we couldn't have done this without you!"

Then he turned to the crowd and hollered with his hands held high. His victory-shout became lost in the roar of the spectators. The howling mob intensified as a great, golden trophy was brought to the stage. It stood nearly as tall as Borzun and at the base was a cloth pouch filled with golden coins. The main official began gesturing for the crowd to quiet down and after several painstaking minutes they were finally silenced.

"As is customary," the official cried out, "the champion will now address his new fans with a speech!" The crowd roared with approval and Borzun stepped forward.

"Five days ago," Borzun began, "I was stuck in a worthless job with nowhere to go. But today..." Borzun continued his speech, but I became distracted by two members of the audience. It was Caden and Aila, they were leaning over and whispering to one another. Then they looked up at us, and I saw Caden's heinous grin. Aila left his side and slithered through the mob of entranced listeners.

I tried to get the official's attention but he just made a shushing sound and pushed me away. Looking back, I saw Aila's hand already glowing with magic. I turned to look at Borzun and beheld a terrible sight. In mid-sentence, he swept an arm through the air and a stream of cards spewed from his sleeve. The spectators all gasped in unison and Borzun stopped with his mouth wide open. He gaped at the cards that lay scattered on the ground before him.

"He's a dirty cheater!" Caden shouted and broke the silence.

"What!? No! I didn't cheat!" Borzun yelled in vain.

"We've been duped, swindled, bamboozled!" Said someone from the crowd.

A different kind of roar began to fill the arena as pitchforks and torches seemed to materialize from nowhere.

"Borzun!" I shouted. "Don't you let go of that trophy!" He clung to it for dear life as the angry mob began to herd us out of the arena to some unknown fate.

* * *

"Yarr!" The burly commoner yelled. "Which one first!?"

We all took a glance over our shoulders into the pit. The unpleasant thought of hundreds of beetles crawling on my skin made my stomach churn.

"I say the cheater goes in first!" A woman hollered with her torch raised high.

"Yahh! Send the cheater in!" The mob echoed.

"No, please!" Bozrun shouted back. "I didn't cheat, I swear!"

"To the pit!" They cried.

Borzun looked at me with pleading eyes. "Duncan," I said. "Do something! Use your magic!"

"I... I don't know if I can..." He quavered.

"Well you had better try, otherwise we're finished!" I drew my sword and watched as Duncan began weaving his hands through the air. A blue glow shined from his fingertips and just as I could see the magic being released I pumped my arm in the air and shouted.

"Aha! Stay back!"

Duncan's whole body began to glow and then a cloud of dust shot forth from his feet and covered him from view. The mob gasped and stepped back fearfully. As the smoke and dust cleared, there stood Duncan. But he was no longer a man... he was a sheep!

Blast that wizard! His spell backfired! Rapidly I began searching for other avenues of escape, but a screeching voice interrupted my search.

"Eeee! That one there with the sword 'as

turned 'im into a sheep!" Milton the peasant stepped forward and pointed at me.

"Oh, oh no! Please, no!" The burly peasant buckled at the knees.

"Ba-a-a-ah," Duncan bleated.

"Oh please! Please spare us, we'll do anything!" Another peasant shouted. Borzun and Olivander looked at me inquisitively.

"Um, that—that's right! You'd all better listen up if you don't want to be turned into a snail!" I yelled.

"What!? No he didn't!" Caden emerged from the crowd. "That idiot did it to himself!"

"Tie him up!" I shouted. "And his friends too!" The peasants all looked reluctantly at Caden, Aila and the other two.

"I'll do it," I said, "someone's about to become a toad!" A clamor erupted and within seconds Caden and his team were bound and gagged. I nearly laughed as I saw Caden glaring at me with a rag in his mouth.

"Alright!" I continued. "Now, let us pass! We'll get our steeds and be on our way without any more trouble!" A wide lane formed in the middle of the mob.

"Olivander, get Duncan," I whispered through the side of my mouth. Olivander grabbed Duncan the sheep and carried him underneath a single arm. Duncan bleated again as if protesting, and we began sliding through the crowd. I kept my sword raised in the air and pointed a threatening finger at anyone who looked like they might issue a challenge. Borzun crept behind us, still holding on to the great trophy.

Finally we made it to the stables where Punter and Molly were kept. I climbed on Punter while Borzun leapt onto Molly and secured the trophy.

"Olivander, hand Duncan to me," I said.

"Ba-a-a-ah!" Duncan wiggled as I set him in the saddle.

"Now what?" Olivander whispered.

"Now we run!" I slapped the mule's haunch and Borzun took off while Olivander followed closely. "Punter, fly!" We sped around the mob and weaved through lanes of houses. The villagers exploded into a tumult as we fled from Berrysboro with as much haste as we could muster.

Chapter 14

RETURN TO CASTLETOWN

We traveled tirelessly back to the King – I knew that Caden and his friends would have escaped their bindings and may catch up to us at any moment. For twenty hours we rode as quickly as we could. As we neared the point of exhaustion, Castletown finally came into view.

My knees buckled and I grabbed Punter's saddle to stabilize as I dismounted before the great hall of King Junip's castle. As we entered the courtyard, Borzun held the trophy and Olivander had Duncan, who was still a sheep, set on top of his shoulders.

A knight permitted us to enter the throne room of King Junip. The low, red light was almost enough to put me to sleep. The door behind the throne burst open and King Junip sprang out from behind its open frame. A feeling of triumph filled me as the King smiled and began laughing joyfully.

"Aha! You did it! I knew you wouldn't let me down! May I see it?" He grabbed the trophy from Borzun and hugged it. "I'm going to set it right here next to my throne. See, doesn't it look good there? Then next year you can win me another one and I'll put it on the other side! Then the year after that you can win again, and the next year you'll win again! Then my throne room will be lined with trophies!"

Borzun and Olivander appeared surprised – I had forgotten they weren't yet acquainted with the antics of the King.

"But forgive me!" The King shouted. "I forget my manners! I am King Junip the Thirteenth, and who might you be master dwarf?" He asked as he gestured toward Borzun.

Borzun removed his glasses and bowed low. "King Junip, I am Borzun from the country of Dwelvon, and this is my elf-brother, Olivander."

King Junip's eyes widened as he elevated his

eyes to meet Olivander's. "Really? An elf, you say? My, my, my... for an elf, you're so incredibly large!"

Borzun's eyes shifted immediately to the stone floor and he shuffled his feet. King Junip blinked several times in the present silence.

"Yes, my King," Olivander finally gulped, "I suppose I am." He sighed and I thought I saw his elven ears lower just barely.

King Junip, aware of his error, opened his mouth to say something. But before he could form a response the great doors to the throne room burst inward with a boom. Caden and his companions thundered down the rows of pillars.

"Oh boy..." I heard Borzun mutter under his breath.

"Follow my lead," I whispered. "We didn't do anything wrong!"

"Hail, King Junip!" Caden knelt before the king and rested his sword point on the stone floor, holding the hilt and pommel before his bowed head.

"Ah, wonderful!" King Junip clapped his hands. "My second troupe of adventurers arrives... trophy *not* in hand, eh!" The King nudged me with his elbow.

"My King, it pains me to say it, but our quest was sabotaged by this band of miscreants!"

Caden sheathed his sword and pointed at us aggressively.

"Oh dear…" King Junip rubbed his smooth chin.

"King Junip," I said, "I assure you these accusations are false! We won that trophy fairly! Our methods were honorable!"

"Bah!" Caden waved his hand. "They deceive you! They left the town in a riot and had us unjustly bound and gagged. Send a message to the Earl of Berrysboro! He will tell you!"

"That is not how it happened!" I protested. But before anyone could speak further, the throne room doors were flung open once more with a heavy thud. A lanky man with a feather in his hat strode forward. Two guards were at his side.

"G-r-r-eat, King Junip!" The man bowed so low that his pointed nose nearly touched the floor. "I am in the employ of Baron Bulgar of the Palm Gates of Dwelvon! It is with great displeasure that I come before you today to apprehend these two vagabonds!" He gestured toward Olivander and Borzun.

"They have fled the estate of Baron Bulgar, yet they owe him still more than 200 gold pieces. By decree of the Baron, they are ordered to be returned to Dwelvon at once and imprisoned in the city dungeon."

The King allowed a short, sharp inhale before he held his breath and glanced back and forth between our accusers. Then his mouth opened wide as if to speak. But again before the words escaped him, a loud crack and a poof filled the throne room. Swirling smoke flowed about, obstructing my vision.

I uncovered my eyes as the smoke cleared. Before us all there stood a regal, elderly man with a great, grey beard – he was garbed in a deep purple robe with silver moons and stars printed on it. Next to him there was a middle-aged woman with a tight bun of brown hair – she was wearing a vibrant, orange robe decorated with swirling flames. The man had a gentle face and half-spectacles that sat on the end of his crooked nose, while the woman had rigid, chiseled features and thick eyebrows. Each of them held a glowing, ornate staff.

King Junip held a hand to his mouth and coughed before he finally erupted. "Alright, alright! Now what, eh!? What is the meaning of this?"

"King Junip," The woman said in a pompous and shrill voice. "I am Grand Mistress Fredsel, and this is my counterpart—"

"I know who he is!" King Junip snapped. "He

lives in Castletown and handles all my magical business. Don't you think I know his name already?"

"Well pardon me!" The woman shrieked. "If I may proceed, O' King, for the sake of those who don't know, this is Archmage Fardron."

"Good afternoon," the old man bowed. King Junip crossed his arms and frowned as he waited for her to proceed.

"We are here to detain that sheep!" She pointed at Duncan and he lowered his sheep ears and took several steps back until he was hidden behind Olivander.

"What kind of tomfoolery is this!?" The King exclaimed. "You burst into my throne room and make such a disturbance for a sheep?"

"Ahem," I stepped forward, "If I may, your highness. This is our wizard-friend, Duncan. He… er, cleverly transformed himself into a sheep to assist in our mission at Berrysboro. However, he seems to be unable to turn back into a man at the moment."

The King's frown slowly diminished until he burst out in laughter. "Haha! Is that so? Well done, well done! What a splendid story!" The King continued to laugh for a good while, apparently very amused by Duncan's predicament. Then he approached Duncan and rubbed his head, flopping Duncan's ears back and forth.

"So, Mr. Duncan the sheep, I have you to thank for my wonderful trophy, eh?" The Grand Mistress thrust forward her staff and magic flew from its crest. Swirling blue light imbued Duncan and within seconds he was a man again. The King turned and frowned at her.

"That poor, excuse for a wizard was ordered to be stripped of his power due to incompetence! But he fled from the ceremony of his dispossession and has further disgraced himself! We demand that he be turned over at once to stand trial for his crime."

King Junip's frown turned to a grimace at her final words. His left eye twitched and he bared his teeth at her.

"You," he shouted "will *demand* nothing from your King! And that goes for you too!" He pointed vigorously at Baron Bulgar's messenger. "Regardless of their past, they have proved themselves worthy to be my champions and will be treated as such! Now, be gone, all of you!"

"Ehrm, good King," Archmage Fardron spoke in a calm tone. "I'm afraid I must protest for your own safety. That wizard is a danger to those—"

"Fardron, I respectfully disagree! This wizard is guilty of nothing but a rather amusing success story! He's exactly the man I need on my team. Now, good day to you all!" King Junip flared his cape as he sat in his throne and clasped his hands together.

Grand Mistress Fredsel looked as though she was about to burst out in anger. But for now she held her peace and disappeared along with Archmage Fardron in another cloud of smoke.

"Mighty one," said Bulgar's messenger. "We are forever your servants and are grateful for your leadership." He stepped right next to Borzun and Olivander and bowed to the King once again.

"If there ever is anything my lord the Baron can do for you, O' King, he would be happy to assist." Then he turned and whispered to my companions.

"You two may be safe for now, but mark my words, *no one* escapes a debt from Baron Bulgar. We'll be seeing you *very* soon." Then he and his convoy marched out of the room without looking back. King Junip slouched in his great chair as they exited.

"Now then..." the King sighed. "That just leaves this small matter between the two of you."

I held my tongue and hoped that Caden would choose his words poorly. After several awkward moments I looked at him and saw that he stared at me with a wry smile. Caden may have been a royal nuisance, but he wasn't stupid – it was clear that he was waiting for me to speak as well.

"Well come on then," said the King. "Someone must speak…"

Another silent moment passed.

"Alright then, you there," he said, pointing at me. "The accused typically speaks first. What have you got to say?"

"I, er, well my King…"

"My Lord," Olivander graciously stepped forward. "We stand by what Quinn has told you and we trust your judgment. May you do what seems best to you."

King Junip smiled and looked toward Caden, who merely nodded his head in silent agreement.

"Well then," said the King. "If neither of you have anything more to say then I find it impossible to decide at this point. So, you will both remain under contract and shall stay in my castle for now. Things will become clear soon enough, I think…"

"My King," said Caden, "It is as you say. It will soon become clear who should remain in your service." Then he unsheathed his sword again and twirled it before catching it in a combat-ready posture. The rest of his group followed suit. It pained me to think it, but they were a dazzling sight in their bright armor and shining robes.

"We are the Gilded Shield Questing Company, and we are at your service! We will show you that these buffoons are not even worthy of the sackcloth tabard he wore as a child!" Caden looked toward me and sheathed his sword with a skillful flourish.

Years of anger welled up inside me and churned with my proud victory. Together they struck a harmonious chord within my chest and I stepped out in that confidence.

As I began to speak, the King smiled and clapped his hands lightly. The growing rivalry seemed to amuse him. "King Junip," I said. "It took more than shining armor and silver thread to win that tournament for you, and we will prove that we have what it takes."

I turned and looked at my companions – Borzun straightened his glasses and leaned against his staff, while Olivander crossed his giant arms and spat to the side. Duncan hefted his great, magical tome under his arm. In our own way, I thought that we too were a sight to behold.

"We are proud of who we are and where we come from!" I said as I turned back to the King and puffed out my chest. "We are the Sackcloth

Heroes of Juniper! And it will be an honor to serve you!"

End of Book 1

Turn the page for a sneak peek of Book 2: *The Fires of Crater Lake* – Coming Soon!

FOREWARNING

I walked alone on a hillside of soft, amber brush. A stream softly babbled to my right, reflecting orange sunrays on its shimmering surface. The sunset sank lower and lower, turning the sky into a beautiful tapestry of color. Looking at myself in the stream's reflection, I felt out of place in my fine, blue tunic. I ruffled my combed hair and smiled.

That's a little better.

Lying on my back near the stream, I took a moment to study the clouds. They drifted lazily across the purple sky, changing color as they slid closer to the fading sun.

"Quinn..."

"Who's there?" I sat upright and looked behind me, but saw no one.

"Quinn... have you forgotten?" Came the voice. It reminded me of the old fortuneteller that I met in Berrysboro, but *something* was different about it.

"Forgotten what? Who's there?"

"Hello, Quinn," it came almost as a whisper. Yet it was loud, as if someone spoke directly into my ear.

"Ah!" A startled gasp escaped. There, standing next to me was a cloaked figure. From beneath the shadowy hood, I could barely make out a strong jaw and an unmoving smile.

"Forgive me," he said. "I didn't mean to frighten you."

"Oh, eh... frighten? No, no... you didn't frighten me." I fidgeted nervously.

The man's smile broadened only slightly. "Good. Will you walk with me, Quinn?"

"Uh, well sure, I suppose," I slowly approached his side. "D'ya mind me asking who you are, though?"

"Mind? No, of course I don't mind. Though, I also won't tell you. That's not important right now."

As I neared him he reached out an arm to

touch my shoulder. As I felt his rough fingertips on my back, the roaring, red dragon flashed before my eyes once more. It came and went in a fraction of a second. I rubbed my eyes and stared at the ground, wondering if I actually saw it again or if I was only remembering the fortuneteller's vision.

"Are you alright, Quinn?" asked the cloaked man as we walked onward.

"What? Oh, yes – I think so."

"Good, you'll need all your wits about you for your coming adventure."

"How do you know about—"

"About Crater Lake? There are many things I know about you, Quinn Alvaret." He turned and looked at me. When he spoke my name, the words seemed bathed in tempered rage.

I took a step back and my hand naturally fell to the hilt of my sword.

"Don't worry," he seemed to notice my defensive reflex. "I'm here to deliver a warning, as a friend. Crater Lake is a dangerous place, Quinn. Not many have ventured there, and with good reason. Inside the collapsed volcano, the lava rivers that flow are so hot, that coming even within 10 feet of them is enough to ignite your clothing."

He resumed walking and I timidly followed.

"Do you have much experience with fire?" He asked.

"No, I can't say that I have."

"Hmm…" he paused again. "Fire is a strange thing, Quinn. It grows, breaths and lives just like you do. We might think that fire is only here to give us warmth on a cold, winter night. It's then, when we're *comfortable* with it – maybe even comfortable enough to rest our eyes for a moment – that we wake from our slumber and find that its appetite grew while we slept.

Within minutes, the very thing we trust for our warmth and comfort can consume everything we love. Get used to the way the fire feels while you're in Crater Lake, Quinn."

He raised his head and I saw his skin that was rough, bronze and almost scaly. His eyes burned like embers.

"Soon…" he continued, "soon fire will be ALL YOU KNOW!" Flames surrounded him only for a brief moment and I heard the dragon roar again. I fell backward and clumsily unsheathed my sword. But the fire subsided and he was nowhere to be found.

Still seated, I turned to behold the hillside I rested in. It no longer flourished with life and nature – it was charred and blackened. Behind the river, fires 50 feet high raged. Without fully knowing why, my eyes filled with tears and sadness overwhelmed me.

Thanks for reading!

Please write a review on Amazon.com – your feedback means more than you know!

To contact the author, email
blakeverboom@gmail.com

Visit us on facebook to subscribe to our email list and receive information regarding future book releases, giveaways, promotions and more!

https://www.facebook.com/SackclothHeroes/

Made in the USA
San Bernardino, CA
14 May 2019